ALFIE

WORDS & PICTURES BY

FRED HARSH

Ideals Children's Books • Nashville, Tennessee

Published by Ideals Publishing Corporation
Nashville, Tennessee 37210

Printed and bound in the United States of America

Library of Congress Cataloging-in-Publication Data

Harsh, Fred.
   Alfie / by Fred Harsh.
     p. cm.
   Summary: Alfie, a baby crow raised by Mr. Orlowski and his dog
Sir Lancelot, believes he is a dog too, until one day he sees himself
reflected in a pond.
   ISBN 0-8249-8513-3
   [1. Crows—Fiction. 2. Dogs—Fiction. 3. Friendship—Fiction.
4. Identity—Fiction.] Title.
PZ7.H25624A1   1991
[E]—dc   91-10121
                                                          CIP
                                                           AC

The illustrations in this book
were rendered in ink and watercolors.
The text type was set in condensed Garamond.
The display type was set in Goudy Handtooled.
Color separations were made by Web Tech, Inc.,
Butler, Wisconsin.
Printed and bound by Arcata Graphics Kingsport,
Kingsport, Tennessee.

For Sarah

The rain began as Mr. Orlowski and his dog, Sir Lancelot, started home from the fields. Soon the branches of the trees waved like great arms in the wind, and the rain swept over the truck in sheets.

Bouncing along the road, the truck passed under a large elm tree. Mr. Orlowski didn't notice the small, black ball of feathers falling from the tree and into the back of his truck.

The next morning, the storm had passed. Mr. Orlowski and Sir Lancelot were going back to the fields when they discovered a very frightened baby crow shivering inside an old shoe in the back of the truck.

"Well, well, what do we have here?" asked Mr. Orlowski. "Not much more than a handful of feathers."

Mr. Orlowski carried the shoe with the shivering bird inside to a warm spot next to the wood stove in the kitchen. For the next few weeks, Mr. Orlowski fed him little crumbs of cornbread and drops of water.

Slowly the little crow forgot about nests and tall trees, and he felt very much at home in that old shoe by the warm fire.

One morning, Mr. Orlowski decided that the little crow should have a name. "Hmmmmm, let's see," he said. "My cousin Alfie came by one stormy night just to visit and stayed for a whole year. That's it!" he exclaimed. "Welcome to the farm, Alfie!"

Little Alfie liked Sir Lancelot right away. He liked to snuggle up to this big, friendly dog when the nights were cool. Soon Sir Lancelot started sharing his dry dog food and his water dish with the little crow.

Alfie followed Sir Lancelot around the house and out into the farmyard.

On longer trips out into the cornfields, he rode on Sir Lancelot's broad back. He didn't know that someday he would fly.

That someday came quite suddenly. One day, Sir Lancelot charged off after a rabbit and left the startled Alfie flapping in mid-air.

"Hey!" he crowed. "Just look at me now!"

From then on, Alfie swooped, soared, and hovered from treetop to rooftop and from Sir Lancelot's back to Mr. Orlowski's shoulder.

One of Sir Lancelot's jobs on the farm was to chase the wild crows out of Mr. Orlowski's cornfield. When they landed by the hundreds, Sir Lancelot would run between the corn rows barking as loud as he could.

"RAURRRRF, RAURRRRF, RAURRRRF."

Alfie rode along on Sir Lancelot's back and, surprisingly, barked as loud as he could, too!

"RAURRRRF, RAURRRRF, RAURRRRF."

How foolish they are, Alfie thought. *Don't those silly crows know that Sir Lancelot and I aren't going to let them eat Mr. Orlowski's corn?*

All that summer, when flocks of crows swooped down on the cornfields, the sounds of barking could be heard throughout the hills and fields.

One day, Mr. Orlowski brought Alfie a fine gift—a tiny red collar just like Sir Lancelot's. A shiny gold tag, engraved with Alfie's name, hung from the collar.

Alfie was happily surprised . . . and very, very proud.

He could only flap his wings and say, "RAURRRRF, RAURRRRF, RAURRRRF," while perched on top of Mr. Orlowski's head.

One day in late summer,
everything changed. After a
long, hard day of chasing crows, Alfie sailed down to drink
from a quiet pond near the cornfield. As he looked down
into the water, a large crow looked back at him.

"RAURRRRF, RAURRRRF," barked Alfie. The crow didn't
move. Again, "RAURRRRF, RAURRRRF." Still no movement.

Strange, thought Alfie. *What kind of crow is this? Doesn't he know he's supposed to be frightened and fly away?*

Then Alfie saw the red collar with the little gold tag. And he knew immediately that it was his very own collar. That meant only one thing.

Alfie was not a dog like Sir Lancelot after all. He was a crow!

He thought about his discovery for a long time. *Now what am I going to do? I can't scare crows anymore—it wouldn't be right. And what are Mr. Orlowski and Sir Lancelot going to think when they find out that I am a crow?*

He flew back to the farmhouse and perched on the top of an old elm tree. He would try his very best to be a crow.

Mr. Orlowski grew worried about Alfie when he noticed that he didn't chase crows with Sir Lancelot anymore. He also noticed when Alfie stopped eating dry dog food and began eating from the corncrib near the barn.

And Alfie didn't bark anymore. He just perched quietly, high up in the old elm tree.

The summer came to an end, the crows went where crows go in cold weather, and the empty cornfields were readied for next year's crop. The farm settled in for the long winter.

Mr. Orlowski could not stop worrying. "I don't know what could be wrong with Alfie," he said to Sir Lancelot. "Our good friend is very unhappy. I wish I knew what to do."

Later that week, Mr. Orlowski and Sir Lancelot went out in the fields to mend fences, and Alfie sat as usual at the top of the old elm.

When he first saw the sparks coming out of the chimney, he didn't pay very much attention. When the sparks fell on the roof and little wisps of smoke blew away with the wind, he looked again. When the little fingers of fire darted over the shingles, Alfie flew into action.

I must get Mr. Orlowski, he thought. *And quick.*

Across the large field Sir Lancelot heard the sound first. From far off in the distance came a familiar noise.

"RAURRRRF, RAURRRRF, RAURRRRF!"

Sir Lancelot's big ears flew up and he answered.

"RAURRRRF, RAURRRRF, RAURRRRF!"

Alfie swooped down flapping and barking. Then he turned and sped back toward the farmhouse.

"Something is wrong at the farmhouse," shouted Mr. Orlowski. "Let's go, Sir Lancelot!"

Minutes later they arrived at the house in a cloud of dust. Mr. Orlowski knew what to do immediately. He grabbed the garden hose and a ladder. Turning on the faucet, he sprang to the roof and put out the fire. Alfie and Sir Lancelot were still barking.

"Okay, you two. It's all over. Let's go inside," Mr. Orlowski said.

Later Mr. Orlowski relaxed at the table while Alfie and Sir Lancelot curled up by the warm stove.

"Alfie," he said, "you did a very fine job. I carelessly left the stove burning too fast, and we would have lost the house if you hadn't warned us. I'm very proud of you.

"And," he added, "I hope you stay with us for a long, long time."

Alfie could think of only one thing to say.

"RAURRRRF, RAURRRRF, RAURRRRF!"

Not bad for a crow, he thought.